FE

The purchase of this item was made possible by a collection development money award by the 2007 Nevada Legislature.

Help for Dear Dragon

by Margaret Hillert
Illustrated by David Helton

NORWOOD HOUSE PRESS

DEAR CAREGIVER, The *Beginning-to-Read* series is a carefully written collection of classic readers you may remember from your own childhood. Each book features text comprised of common sight words to provide your child ample practice reading the words that appear most frequently in written text. The many additional details in the pictures enhance the story and offer the opportunity for you to help your child expand oral language and develop comprehension.

Begin by reading the story to your child, followed by letting him or her read familiar words and soon your child will be able to read the story independently. At each step of the way, be sure to praise your reader's efforts to build his or her confidence as an independent reader. Discuss the pictures and encourage your child to make connections between the story and his or her own life. At the end of the story, you will find reading activities and a word list that will help your child practice and strengthen beginning reading skills.

Above all, the most important part of the reading experience is to have fun and enjoy it!

Shannon Cannon

Shannon Cannon,
Literacy Consultant

Norwood House Press • P.O. Box 316598 • Chicago, Illinois 60631
For more information about Norwood House Press please visit our website at *www.norwoodhousepress.com* or call 866-565-2900.

LIBRARY OF CONGRESS CATALOGING-IN-PUBLICATION DATA
    Hillert, Margaret.
     Help for dear dragon / by Margaret Hillert ; illustrated by David
Helton.—Rev. and expanded library ed.
       p. cm. — (Beginning to read series. Dear dragon)
     Summary: When "dear dragon" feels sick, he receives help from a friendly
veterinarian. Includes reading activities.
     ISBN-13: 978-1-59953-019-2 (library edition : alk. paper)
     ISBN-10: 1-59953-019-8 (library edition : alk. paper)
     [1. Veterinarians—Fiction. 2. Dragons—Fiction. 3. Readers.] I. Helton, David, ill.
II. Title. III. Series.
    PZ7.H558He 2006
    [E]—dc22
                            200503351

Beginning-to-Read series © 2006 by Margaret Hillert.
Library edition published by permission of Pearson Education, Inc. in arrangement
with Norwood House Publishing Company. All rights reserved.

Here you are.
Here is something to eat.
It is what you like.

DRAGON

3

No?
You do not want it?
That is funny.

You did not want to get up.
Now you do not want to eat.
You do not look good.
What is it?
What can I do?

You are not happy.
I am not happy.
This is not good.
I have to get help
for you.

Come on now.
Get in here.
We will go for help.

Away we go.
This way.
This way.
You will see.

Here it is.

This is where we want to go.
In here. In here.

11

Oh, my.
Look here—
     and here—
          and here.

WAITING
ROOM

Have you come to
get help, too?
This is a good
spot for it.

Come in.
Come in.
Jump up here.
I want to have a look at you.

I will look down here to
see what I can see.

Oh, oh.

My, you do not look
too good.
Not too good, but I
can help.

I want to look at this, too.
I want to find out something
with this.

Now I will do this.
This will be a big
help to you.

Yes, yes.
This is good for you.
And you are a good
little dragon.

Here is something red.
I want you to have this too.
It is something that will help.

Now you can get down.
Down,
   down,
      down.

And away you go.
You will want to eat now.
You will want to
run and play.

Come on. Come on.
Run, run, run.
I will get you something
good to eat.

Here you are.
Eat it up, and we will
go out to play.
What fun we will have!

Here you are with me.
And here I am with you.
Now it is a happy day, dear dragon.

READING REINFORCEMENT

The following activities support the findings of the National Reading Panel that determined the most effective components for reading instruction are: Phonemic Awareness, Phonics, Vocabulary, Fluency, and Text Comprehension.

Phonemic Awareness: The /h/ sound

Deletion: Ask your child to say the following words without the beginning /**h**/ sound:

hat - /h/ = at   hop - /h/ = op   ham - /h/ = am
hit - /h/ = it   his - /h/ = is   harm - /h/ = arm
hand - /h/ = and   hair - /h/ = air

Phonics: The letter Hh

1. Demonstrate how to form the letters **H** and **h** for your child.

2. Have your child practice writing **H** and **h** at least three times each.

3. Ask your child to point to the words in the book that start with the letter **h**.

4. Write down the following words and ask your child to circle the letter **h** in each word:

happy	hand	mother	hug
help	father	home	how
hair	the	there	here
hut	house	where	have

Vocabulary: Be the Words

1. Write the following words on separate pieces of paper:

   cough   cold   stomach ache

   sore throat   sneeze   fever

2. Say each word and ask your child to act it out.

3. Act out each word and ask your child to point to the correct word(s).

Fluency: Choral Reading

1. Reread the story to your child at least two more times while your child tracks the print by running a finger under the words as they are read. Ask your child to read the words he or she knows with you.

2. Reread the story aloud together. Be careful to read at a rate that your child can keep up with.

3. Repeat choral reading and allow your child to be the lead reader and ask him or her to change from a whisper to a loud voice while you follow along and change your voice.

Text Comprehension: Discussion Time

1. Ask your child to retell the sequence of events in the story.

2. To check comprehension, ask your child the following questions:

   • Where did the boy take Dear Dragon?

   • How did the boy know Dear Dragon needed help?

   • Describe a time when you were sick. Who helped you and how?

WORD LIST

Help for Dear Dragon uses the 67 words listed below.
This list can be used to practice reading the words that appear in the text.
You may wish to write the words on index cards and use them to help your
child build automatic word recognition. Regular practice with these words
will enhance your child's fluency in reading connected text.

a	eat	jump	see
all	find	like	something
am	for	little	spot
and	fun	look	
are	funny		that
at		me	this
away	get	my	to
	go		too
be	good	no	
big		not	up
but	happy	now	
	have		want
can	help	oh	way
come	here	on	we
	how	out	what
day			where
dear	I	play	will
did	in	red	with
do	is	run	
down	it		yes
dragon			you

ABOUT THE AUTHOR Margaret Hillert has written over 80 books for
children who are just learning to read. Her books
have been translated into many different languages and over a million children
throughout the world have read her books. She first started writing poetry as
a child and has continued to write for children and adults throughout her life. A
first grade teacher for 34 years, Margaret is now retired from teaching and lives in
Michigan where she likes to write, take walks in the morning, and care for her three cats.

Photograph by Glenna Washburn

ABOUT THE ADVISER Shannon Cannon contributed the activities pages that appear in
this book. Shannon serves as a literacy consultant and provides
staff development to help improve reading instruction. She is a frequent presenter at educational
conferences and workshops. Prior to this she worked as an elementary school teacher and as
president of a curriculum publishing company.